THE DIAMOND HEIST AT THE ANCIENT MUSEUM OF CHANDRAPUR

THE CHRONICLES OF DETECTIVE UNIVERSE

APPALLA YAZNA SURYA SAI KIRAN

Made with ♥ on the Notion Press Platform
www.notionpress.com

To my beloved family,

Without your unwavering support and encouragement, this novel would not have been possible. Thank you for always believing in me and cheering me on through the ups and downs of this creative journey.

This novel, "The Diamond Heist at the Ancient Museum of Chandrapur," is a testament to the love and inspiration you have given me throughout my life. Your love has been a diamond that has shone brightly, guiding me through even the darkest of times.

I dedicate this book to you, my dear family, as a token of my gratitude and love. May this novel bring you as much joy and excitement as you have brought into my life.

With all my love and appreciation,

A.Y.S. SAI KIRAN

Contents

About Author

A.Y.S. Sai Kiran is a passionate writer from India. Sai Kiran has always had a love for language and storytelling. Starting from an early age, Sai Kiran has written short stories and poetry and has now published a novel.

Sai Kiran's writing style is heavily influenced by Indian culture and mythology, with a touch of magic realism. Sai Kiran is also an avid reader and draws inspiration from authors such as Salman Rushdie, Jhumpa Lahiri, Kommuri Sambhasivarao, Madhubabu, and Arundhati Roy. When not writing, Sai Kiran enjoys traveling and exploring new cultures.

About The Book

PREVIOUS BOOKS

CBI Chronicles: The Cases of Officer Ranjit

Saving India from Nuclear Doom: The Sardar Story

Foreword

Dear Reader,

I am thrilled to present to you my latest novel, "The Diamond Heist at the Ancient Museum of Chandrapur." Get ready for an adrenaline-fueled ride as you follow our daring protagonist through the twists and turns of this thrilling heist. I hope this story keeps you on the edge of your seat from start to finish.

Enjoy the adventure!

A.Y.S. SAI KIRAN

Preface

"The Diamond Heist at the Ancient Museum of Chandrapur" is a work of fiction inspired by my fascination with heist stories and ancient history. Through this novel, I invite you to join me on a journey that explores the human psyche, greed, and the consequences of our actions. I hope you enjoy reading this story as much as I enjoyed writing it.

A.Y.S. Sai Kiran

Acknowledgements

I would like to express my heartfelt gratitude to my family and friends for their constant support and encouragement during the writing process of "The Diamond Heist at the Ancient Museum of Chandrapur." I also extend my sincere appreciation to my editor, beta readers, and everyone who helped me bring this novel to life. Thank you for your invaluable contributions.

A.Y.S. Sai Kiran

Prologue

The ancient museum of Chandrapur is home to the world's most exquisite and valuable diamond, the "Chandrapur Diamond." But when a group of thieves targets the museum in a daring heist, everything changes. Join our protagonist as they navigate through the murky world of crime, deception, and danger to uncover the truth behind the heist and reclaim the diamond.

A.Y.S. Sai Kiran

Attention Note

Dear Readers,

I am thrilled to present my novel, which is entirely a work of fiction. All characters, events, and locations in this book are the product of my imagination and have no relation to real-life people or places.

From the vibrant city of Nayakpur to the intricate world of espionage and crime, this novel takes you on a journey through a fictional world that I have created. I hope you enjoy getting lost in this world, as much as I enjoyed crafting it.

Thank you for taking the time to read my work, and I hope it brings you joy and entertainment.

Sincerely, A.Y.S. SAI KIRAN

The Chronicles Of Detective Universe

In "The Chronicles of Detective Universe," readers are taken on an exciting journey through the world of Indian espionage and crime. Follow the adventures of an Indian spy, a detective, and a CBI officer as they navigate through complex cases and fight to protect their country.

When an epic threat looms over India, the three major characters find themselves in an unexpected situation, working together to stop the imminent danger. With their combined skills, they embark on a dangerous mission to save their country from destruction.

As they work tirelessly to unravel the mystery behind the threat, they face numerous obstacles and challenges that put their lives on the line. But with their unwavering determination and commitment to their country, they press on, determined to succeed.

With its fast-paced action, intricate plotlines, and compelling characters, "The Chronicles of Detective Universe" is a thrilling series that will keep you on the edge of your seat until the very end. Follow the journey of the Indian spy, detective, and CBI officer as they fight to protect their country and bring justice to the victims of crime.

CHAPTER ONE

The Diamond Heist at the Ancient Museum of Chandrapur

The Chronicles Of Detective Universe

CHAPTER TWO

Queen Aisha Museum of Historical Treasures.

The Queen Aisha Museum of Historical Treasures is a premier destination for history and art lovers alike. It was established to showcase the rich cultural heritage of Chandrapur and its surrounding regions. Housed within its walls are priceless artifacts and artworks, many of which date back to the ancient Indo-British period. From intricately carved sculptures to glittering jewels and coins, this museum is a true treasure trove of history and culture. With its stunning architecture and carefully curated exhibitions, the Queen Aisha Museum is a must-visit destination for anyone who appreciates the beauty and significance of ancient art and artifacts.

Additionally, the museum boasts state-of-the-art security measures to protect its priceless collections. Its experienced curators and tour guides are available to provide expert insights and background information on the many fascinating pieces on display. With its welcoming atmosphere and commitment to preserving the past for future generations, the Queen Aisha Museum of Historical Treasures is a true gem of Chandrapur. Whether you're a history buff, an art aficionado, or simply a lover of beauty and culture, this museum is sure to captivate and inspire you.

The museum is a hub for research and academic study, hosting numerous conferences, workshops, and lectures throughout the year. It also has a robust educational program for students, with interactive exhibits, guided tours, and hands-on activities designed to bring history to life. The museum also features a well-stocked library and archives, containing a wealth of information on the many civilizations and cultures represented in its collections. Whether you're an expert or a novice, the Queen Aisha Museum of Historical Treasures offers a wealth of opportunities to deepen your knowledge and appreciation of the rich tapestry of human history.

CHAPTER THREE

Star of the East aka Empress jewel

The Diamond of Queen Aisha, also known as the Star of the East, is a magnificent gemstone that dates back to the reign of the Indo-British Queen Aisha. It is said to have been mined from the foothills of the Himalayas and was a symbol of wealth, power, and prosperity for the queen and her kingdom. The diamond is a cut solitaire, weighing approximately 50 carats, and boasts a rich, golden hue that shimmers like the sun. It was considered one of the greatest treasures of the queen's reign and was passed down from generation to generation, eventually making its way to the Queen Aisha Museum of Historical Treasures in Chandrapur. The diamond is one of the museum's most prized possessions and is displayed in a specially designed glass case, surrounded by detailed documentation of its history and significance.

The Empress's Jewel, also known as the "Star of the East," is a legendary diamond said to have once belonged to an Indo-British queen. Its unique blend of size and clarity, combined with its rich history, has made it one of the most sought-after gems in the world. With its home at the ancient museum in Chandrapur, the Empress's Jewel is an enduring symbol of the city's rich cultural heritage, attracting visitors from near and far. However, its value also makes it a target for thieves, leading to heightened security measures at the museum.

The story of the Empress's Jewel dates back centuries, to a time when the Indo-British queen ruled her kingdom with grace and power. According to legend, she wore the diamond in a crown as a symbol of her rule and her people's prosperity. Over time, the diamond passed down through the generations, becoming a symbol of the royal family's wealth and prestige.

When the last of the Indo-British queens passed away, the diamond was donated to the museum in Chandrapur, where it has been displayed for the public to admire ever since. Despite its secure location within the museum, the Empress's Jewel has been the target of numerous theft attempts over the years. Each time, the heists have been foiled, allowing the diamond to remain a symbol of the city's rich cultural heritage.

Today, the Empress's Jewel remains one of the most valuable and sought-after gems in the world. It is not only a symbol of Indo-British royalty but also a testament to the perseverance and strength of the museum in Chandrapur, which has successfully safeguarded the diamond for so many years.

CHAPTER FOUR

The Diamond Heist at the Ancient Museum of Chandrapur

The city of Chandrapur was home to one of the most prestigious museums of antiquities in the country, and it was a source of pride for the citizens of Chandrapur. The museum was renowned for its collection of rare and valuable artifacts, including the "Empress's Jewel," a diamond-encrusted crown that was said to have belonged to a powerful ancient queen.

However, one day, the city was rocked by news of a daring diamond heist at the museum. The thieves had made off with millions of dollars in diamonds, including the "Empress's Jewel." The police were at a loss as to how they had managed to penetrate the museum's sophisticated security system.

It was the night of CBI officer Ranjit's marriage, and he was looking forward to spending his first night as a married man with his new wife. However, the peace was shattered when he received an urgent call from the CBI office. The ancient museum in Chandrapur had been robbed, and the thieves had made off with millions of dollars in diamonds, including the legendary "Empress's Jewel." Despite his protests, Ranjit was tasked with leading the investigation into the daring heist. With a heavy heart, he said goodbye to his bride and set out to solve the case.

Ranjit, being the dedicated CBI officer that he is, immediately left his bride and headed to the museum. As he arrived at the scene, he was met with the daunting task of finding the culprit behind the heist.

Upon arriving at the museum, Ranjit found that it was in complete chaos. The museum staff was running around, trying to figure out what had happened. The security system had been breached and the thieves had made off with the Empress's Jewel, along with several other priceless diamonds. The police were on the scene, but so far, they had no leads. The museum's staff were still in shock, and many of them were visibly shaken. As Ranjit began to survey the scene, he knew that this was going to be a challenging case, but he was determined to get to the bottom of it.

When Ranjit arrived at the museum, he immediately went to speak with the staff. He asked the museum manager about the details of the heist and the security measures that were in place at the time of the theft.

The manager told Ranjit that the museum had been closed for the night and that the security cameras had not recorded any unusual activity. He added that the alarm system had not been triggered and that the staff had not noticed anything suspicious when they arrived the next morning.

Ranjit then spoke with the security guard who was on duty the night of the theft. The guard told Ranjit that he had been making rounds every hour and that everything seemed to be in order. He added that he had not seen or heard anything unusual during his shift.

Ranjit took note of all the information and promised the museum staff that he would do everything in his power to bring the thief to justice. He then set out to examine the crime scene and gather evidence, determined to crack the case.

At the museum, Ranjit met with the head curator, who was shaken and visibly upset by the theft. "This is an absolute disaster," the curator said. "The Empress's Jewel was one of the museum's most prized possessions. It was a symbol of our city's rich cultural heritage, and now it's gone."

Ranjit asked if there had been any eyewitnesses to the theft. The curator told him that the museum had only one security guard on duty that night, and he had reported seeing nothing out of the ordinary. However, when they reviewed the security footage, they noticed that one of the cameras had been tampered with.

Ranjit was determined to get to the bottom of this crime. He knew that finding the stolen diamonds was going to be a tough case, but he was up for the challenge. As he left the museum, he couldn't help but think that this was going to be a long night.

After leaving the museum, Ranjit immediately began gathering information and reviewing the museum's blueprint.

Ranjit then went out to speak to any potential witnesses who may have seen something suspicious.

Ranjit headed out of the museum and into the streets, eager to gather as much information as he could about the heist. He approached the neighboring shops, hoping to find any witnesses or information that could help him in his investigation.

The first shop he visited was a small convenience store. The owner, a kind-hearted woman in her sixties, offered Ranjit a cup of tea as he questioned her about the night of the heist.

"Did you see anything strange or unusual that night?" Ranjit asked, taking a sip of his tea.

The woman thought for a moment and then replied, "Well, now that you mention it, I did see a couple of men lurking around the museum just before the alarm went off. They looked suspicious, but I didn't think anything of it at the time."

Ranjit wrote down the details in his notebook and thanked the woman for her help. He continued down the street, visiting more shops and talking to more witnesses.

Ranjit approached another neighboring shop, the owner of a stationery store. The store owner was eager to help, as the museum was a major source of business for the store. When Ranjit asked about the events of the night of the heist, the store owner told him that he had closed up shop early that evening due to a sudden headache. He had gone home and gone to bed early, but he hadn't seen or heard anything out of the ordinary. Despite this lack of information, Ranjit made a mental note of the store owner's name and address for further investigation.

As Ranjit continued his investigation, he decided to speak with another neighboring shop owner, who had a store just a few doors down from the museum. He introduced himself and asked if the shop owner had seen or heard anything unusual on the night of the heist. The shop owner seemed nervous and kept fidgeting with his hands. He told Ranjit that he had been closed for the night and didn't see or hear anything.

However, as the conversation went on, Ranjit started to suspect the shop owner. He noticed that the man's hands were shaking, and he seemed to be avoiding eye contact. Ranjit made a note of his observations and decided to look into the shop owner further.

Ranjit continued to question the third neighboring shop owner, gathering more information about the night of the heist. He was cautious, but friendly in his demeanor, always alert for any signs of guilt or nervousness. As he spoke with the shop owner, he took note of every detail, jotting down any information that seemed important. Suddenly, the shop owner's demeanor changed, and he grew more fidgety and evasive. Ranjit's instincts kicked in, and he suspected that this man knew more about the heist than he was letting on. He made a mental note to keep an eye on this suspect and to question him again at a later time.

During his conversation with the fourth neighboring shop owner, Ranjit learned that the owner had seen a strange vehicle parked near the museum around the time of the heist. The owner had noticed it because it was a luxury car, out of place in the working-class neighborhood. He described the car as a sleek black sports car with tinted windows. He couldn't make out the model, but he was sure that it was expensive and out of place in the neighborhood. Ranjit made note of this information, sensing that it could be a lead in the case.

As Ranjit continued his investigation, he decided to speak with the last neighboring shop owner, a woman who ran a small bakery. As he approached her shop, he noticed that she looked familiar. When he introduced himself, she smiled and exclaimed, "Oh my goodness, you're Ranjit! I remember you from when you were just a little boy. Your mother used to bring you by my shop for treats."

Ranjit was surprised and pleased to see an old friend. They chatted for a while about their families and old times, but eventually, he had to turn the conversation back to the case. He asked her if she had seen anything suspicious on the night of the heist.

The woman thought for a moment and then said, "Well, now that you mention it, I did see a car that I've never seen around here before. It was a sleek, black sports car. I remember thinking it was out of place in this neighborhood."

Ranjit thanked her for her information and made a mental note of the car description. Could this be a significant lead? He couldn't be sure, but he was determined to find out.

After his conversation with the neighboring shop owners, Ranjit was tired and decided to head back home. He was eager to spend some quality time with his newly-wed wife, who had been waiting eagerly for his return. As they caught up on the events of the day, they enjoyed a simple dinner together, making plans for their future as husband and wife. Despite the hectic day and the ongoing investigation, Ranjit couldn't help but feel grateful for the love and support of his wife. They retired to bed, exhausted but content, ready to tackle the challenges of the next day together.

The next day, Officer Ranjit begins his investigation with the leads he gathered from the neighboring shop owners. He and his team searched for the car that was described by the fourth shop owner. They eventually find it in an abandoned area, damaged and with traces of blood inside. This discovery raises new questions and concerns for the CBI team, leading them to dig deeper into their investigation.

The number plate was partially damaged and unreadable, but Ranjit and his team made an effort to try and decode the number. They sent the car to the lab for further examination and to gather any other clues that might help them in their investigation.

Ranjit and his team spent the whole day going through CCTV footage from nearby buildings, trying to find any clues about the stolen diamonds and the suspect car. Despite hours of searching, they couldn't find any signs of suspicious activity. However, they did manage to catch a glimpse of the car in some of the footage taken before the heist took place. This gave them a small lead, but they were still a long way from finding the diamonds and the criminals behind the theft.

Ranjit and his team continued their investigation and focused on the partially seen car number in the CCTV footage. After cross-checking the car number from the crime scene and the partially visible car number from the CCTV footage, Ranjit and his team discovered that the numbers did not match. This was a major setback in their investigation and they had to start from square one again. They couldn't believe their luck, after all their hard work, the lead seemed to have fallen apart. They had to regroup and brainstorm new ways to uncover the truth and find the missing diamonds.

Ranjit and his team of officers were determined to catch the thieves behind the diamond heist at the museum. Despite the partial car number, they were unable to match it with any registered vehicles. They knew that time was of the essence, as the thieves were still at large and could strike again at any moment. They scoured the city for any leads, interviewing witnesses and going over CCTV footage from the night of the heist. It seemed like the thieves had covered their tracks well, but Ranjit was not going to give up. He was determined to bring the perpetrators to justice and recover the stolen diamonds, including the valuable "Empress's Jewel."

After a few days, Ranjit and his team were thrilled to have received a lead in the case of the museum heist. The 53-year-old man had reported that a 25-year-old woman had visited his jewelry shop a week before the heist and bought some jewelry. The woman had asked if he had anything like the

"Empress's Jewel." This was a big breakthrough in the case and Ranjit was eager to follow this lead.

The old man described the woman as having long dark hair, wearing a red dress, and having a noticeable scar above her left eyebrow. He also mentioned that she had a foreign accent but he couldn't place it. Ranjit thanked the old man for the information and promised to keep him updated on the case.

Ranjit and his team went to the jewelry shop and asked for the CCTV footage of the day the unknown woman had visited. They cross-checked the details provided by the old man against the footage and made a note of any similarities or differences. They also questioned the shopkeeper to see if they could provide any additional information about the woman or her behavior. As they gathered more information, they continued to piece together a profile of the potential suspect.

Ranjit and his team carefully observed the CCTV footage of the jewelry shop and noticed that the woman's behavior was indeed suspicious. Although they couldn't directly connect her to the theft, they still considered her actions to be worth investigating further. Ranjit made a note of the woman's appearance and behavior and decided to continue the investigation to see if they could uncover any additional leads.

Ranjit decides to track down Fathima and bring her in for questioning to see if she has any involvement in the theft. He sets a plan in motion to locate her and gather any relevant information that could help in the investigation. Ranjit believes that a thorough examination of Fathima's background and activities could shed some light on the theft case.

interrogation of Fathima begins, ranjit and his team asks her several questions related to the heist and her relation with Dinesh Kumar Yadav, but she denies any involvement in the theft. Further investigation is needed to find the truth.

Ranjit: Can you please tell me about your visit to the jewelry shop a week before the heist?

Fathima: Yes, I was just browsing the shop and I saw some beautiful jewelry there. I just asked if they had any specific designs, like the Empress's Jewel.

Ranjit: Did you buy anything from the shop?

Fathima: No, I didn't like anything there so I left.

Ranjit: Can you tell me about your relationship with Dinesh Kumar Yadav?

Fathima: He was my ex-boyfriend. We broke up a few months ago.

Ranjit: And do you have any involvement with the theft at the jewelry shop?

Fathima: No, I don't. I had nothing to do with that.

Ranjit: Can you please tell me your whereabouts on the day of the heist?

Fathima: I was at home that day. I didn't go anywhere.

Ranjit: Can anyone confirm your alibi?

Fathima: Yes, my roommate was with me all day. She can confirm my whereabouts.

Ranjit: All right, I will need to speak with your roommate. Thank you for your time.

Ranjit entered Fathima's room and saw her roommate sitting on the couch.

Ranjit: Hi, I am Ranjit. Can I speak with you for a moment?

Roommate: Yes, sure. How can I help you?

Ranjit: I am investigating the jewelry heist that happened recently and I came to know that Fathima was here a week before the heist. Can you tell me anything about her behavior or any suspicious activity?

Roommate: Well, I didn't notice anything unusual about her behavior. But she did receive a lot of phone calls and text messages that seemed to make her very nervous.

Ranjit: Can you tell me anything else? Do you remember any specific details about the calls or messages?

Roommate: No, I am sorry I don't remember anything specific. She never talked about her personal life or whom she was talking to on the phone.

Ranjit: All right. Thank you for your time. If you remember anything else, please let me know.

Roommate: Sure, I will.

Ranjit asked Fathima's roommate some questions, but she seemed evasive in her answers. Ranjit became suspicious that she was hiding something. He decided to keep a close eye on her and continue the investigation.

Ranjit was intrigued by the results of the car lab reports from the forensic. The results showed that the blood found in the car had three different blood groups - A, AB, and O. This information made Ranjit think more about the possibility of multiple people being involved in the heist.

Ranjit's investigation hit a dead end with the blood samples not matching any of the known thieves. He needed to find another lead. He decided to go back to the scene of the crime and look for any other evidence that might have been missed earlier. He also re-interviewed some of the witnesses, hoping to uncover some new information. Despite the setbacks, Ranjit was determined to solve the case and bring the thieves to justice.

During his revisit to the museum, Ranjit noticed something unusual. He noticed a discarded cigarette butt which he later identified as a very rare brand. This piqued his interest and he began to investigate further. He questioned the security personnel and the cleaning staff about the cigarette and if they saw anyone smoking it.

Ranjit entered the museum and approached the staff. He asked them about the rare cigarette he had found at the crime scene.

"Excuse me, do any of you smoke this brand of cigarette?" Ranjit asked, showing them the pack.

"No, I've never seen that brand before," one of the staff members said.

"Me neither," another chimed in.

Ranjit continued to question them, "Do any of your colleagues smoke this brand? Maybe someone who was here the day of the heist?"

One of the staff members thought for a moment and said, "There was a security guard who smoked a similar brand, but I don't know if it's the same one. He left a few months ago."

Ranjit made a mental note of the information and thanked the staff for their help. He decided to track down the former security guard and see if he had any information related to the heist.

Ranjit began to investigate the former security guard, who had left his job a few months ago. He discovered that the guard had passed away after leaving his job. Ranjit suspected that the guard could have had some connection to the heist, so he tried to gather more information about the guard's life and work. He talked to the guard's former colleagues, friends, and family members to see if they knew anything that could be related to the heist. He also analyzed the guard's financial records and personal belongings to see if any clues could lead him to the culprits. Despite his efforts, Ranjit was unable to find any concrete evidence that connected the guard to the heist, and he was forced to move on to other leads.

During the investigation of the former security guard, Ranjit found out that the rare cigarette was only manufactured in the city of Nayakpur. This information led him to suspect that the person responsible for the heist might have some connection to the city. He decided to visit Nayakpur and look for more clues and information about the rare cigarette.

Ranjit began his investigation by talking to the residents and shopkeepers in Nayakpur. He showed them pictures of the cigarette and asked if they had seen it before. Some of the shopkeepers recognized the cigarette and told Ranjit that it was a popular brand among the wealthy and elite in the city.

Ranjit also talked to the local tobacco factory owner, who told him that the cigarette was only manufactured for a limited time and was very difficult to find. The owner also mentioned that the cigarette was popular among the city's influential and wealthy residents, who would often trade it as a symbol of their status.

With this new information, Ranjit became convinced that the heist was not just a random crime, but was planned and executed by someone with connections to Nayakpur. He decided to dig deeper and find out more about the city's wealthy residents and their connections to the rare cigarette.

During the investigation, Ranjit decided to visit Nayakpur and interview some of the wealthy residents there. He suspected that the rare cigar might have been acquired by one of these residents and that it could lead him to the thieves.

Ranjit spoke to several residents, including a wealthy businessman and a prominent socialite. He asked about the rare cigar and if they had any information about it. However, none of the residents had any useful information and they all claimed to have never heard of the cigar before.

Frustrated by the lack of progress, Ranjit decided to expand his investigation and speak to more people in the city. He visited local cigar shops, spoke to street vendors, and even knocked on the doors of people who lived near the cigar factory.

Despite his efforts, Ranjit was still unable to find any concrete leads. He was starting to feel like the trail had gone cold and that he might never find the thieves or the stolen jewels. However, he was determined to keep searching and was not ready to give up yet.

he learned about a highly renowned detective by the name of Gurunadam who was known to have solved many difficult cases in the past.

Ranjit was fascinated by the reputation of Gurunadam and decided to visit him. As he reached the detective's office, he was greeted by a bustling crowd of people who were all seeking Gurunadam's assistance with their cases. Despite the busy schedule, Gurunadam was able to spare a few moments to talk to Ranjit.

During the conversation, Ranjit explained to Gurunadam the reason for his visit and the details of the case he was working on. Gurunadam listened intently and offered his insights on the matter. He told Ranjit that the cigar was a specialty brand that was only manufactured in Nayakpur and was highly sought after by cigar connoisseurs.

Gurunadam also informed Ranjit that the cigar was only sold at a select few shops in the city and that it was essential for Ranjit to start his investigation there. The detective suggested that Ranjit speak to the shopkeepers and see if they remembered any suspicious individuals who had purchased the cigar.

Ranjit was grateful for the advice and immediately set out to visit the shops. After speaking to several shopkeepers, he finally found a lead. One of the shopkeepers told him that a man who matched the description of the thief had come in to purchase the cigar a few days before the theft at the museum.

Excited by this new development, Ranjit returned to Gurunadam to inform him of the progress he had made. The detective was impressed by Ranjit's dedication and offered to assist him.

Ranjit visited the detective's office and shared the details of what had happened in Nayakpur. The detective, who was impressed by Ranjit's dedication to solving the case, offered to assist him but mentioned that he was also working on other cases. Despite his workload, the detective listened attentively to Ranjit and offered to help in any way he could.

Detective Gurunadam was assigned an important case and had to leave the office. In the evening, Ranjit also left Nayakpur and returned to his home, where he took some time to rest.

Ranjit, who was working at the CBI office, arranged a meeting with his team. During the meeting, he shared that he had obtained a valuable clue while investigating the case in Nayakpur. He explained that while looking into the cigarette butts found at the scene of the jewelry museum robbery, he had discovered a lead about the person who had purchased the cigarettes. This new information was important in the ongoing investigation, and Ranjit and his team were determined to follow the lead and get closer to solving the case.

Ranjit and his team had received information about the individual who had purchased the cigarettes and left them at the scene of the robbery. This person was described as a man with black hair and cat-like eyes. The most distinctive feature was that he had six fingers on his left hand and a scar above his left eyebrow. This description was crucial in the investigation, as it could help the team identify and track down the suspect. With this information, Ranjit and his team were now one step closer to solving the case and bringing justice to the victims of the jewelry museum robbery.

Ranjit and his team, including team member Sanjay Kumar, were determined to find the person who had purchased the cigarettes and left them at the scene of the jewelry museum robbery. They started by cross-checking the information with the criminal records, but to their disappointment, they did not find any matches. After a few hours, they tried cross-checking the information with public records, but again, they did not find any relevant information. The team became frustrated and irritated as they were not making any progress in the investigation.

However, upon the suggestion of their superiors, they decided to cross-check the information with public and criminal records from other states. After a thorough search, they finally found a match and discovered the identity of the person they were looking for. This was a breakthrough in the investigation and brought the team one step closer to solving the case and bringing justice to the victims of the robbery.

The team discovered that the person they were looking for was named John Abraham and was from Uttar Pradesh. To their surprise, they found that he had no criminal records, and his name was only found in public records. This new information was important as it helped the team to understand more about the suspect and get a better idea of their motives and actions. With this information, Ranjit and his team were now in a better position to solve the case and bring the culprit to justice.

Ranjit and his team started the investigation by interrogating people near the abandoned house. They learned that the house had been abandoned for the past three years, ever since John Abraham's parents had passed away from cancer. With this new information, the team got a lead on where John Abraham worked before his parents died. They went to the paper mill where John had worked and found that it was now a printing press for the Janasainik newspaper. They interrogated the people working at the press, but they were all newly recruited and didn't have any information about John.

Ranjit's team then interrogated the paper mill manager, who was now the owner of the Janasainik newspaper. The manager revealed that John was a very good and humble person who worked very hard. However, after his parents died from cancer, he couldn't bear the loss and left his job. The manager stated that John had become a rogue and stopped coming to work after a few months. He had seen John in Chandrapur with a girl after a year, but he did not meet him and had not seen or heard anything about him until Ranjit's team arrived. Additionally, the manager mentioned that he saw John in Chandrapur's popular hotel, the Empress Hotel. This new piece of information provided another lead for Ranjit's team to follow as they continued their investigation to find John. They now had a new location to search for the suspect and possibly find more information that could lead to his capture.

Upon learning that John was seen at the Empress Hotel in Chandrapur, Ranjit, and his team went there to continue the investigation. Ranjit, the lead detective, interrogated the hotel staff and management to gather information about John. He asked them about his whereabouts, his activities during his stay, and any other relevant details.

Ranjit's questions and demeanor during the interrogation were professional and respectful, as he was trying to gather as much information as possible without compromising the investigation. The staff and management provided whatever information they had, including details about John's room number, the dates of his stay, and any other relevant information they remembered.

Ranjit also searched John's room and went through his belongings to see if there were any clues or evidence that could help the investigation. Based on the information gathered during the interrogation and the examination of John's room, Ranjit was able to piece together a better understanding of John's actions and movements. This information was then used to further the investigation and hopefully lead to John's capture.

During the examination of John's room at the Empress Hotel, Ranjit and his team were able to gather new information about him. However, it is not specified what specific information was obtained. In general, an examination of a suspect's room can reveal many things such as their items, documents, clothing, and other belongings that can provide insight into their life, habits, and possibly their motivations.

It is also possible that they found items that could potentially be used as evidence in the case, such as fingerprints, DNA samples, or any other physical or tangible evidence that could link John to the crime. Whatever information was gathered during this examination was likely used to further the investigation and bring the case closer to a resolution.

they got a new clue in john's room it is a photo of john and an anonymous girl. Ranjit and his team have now found a new lead in the form of a photo of John with a girl named Kumari. They have confirmed that the girl in the photo is the same one seen with John in the past by the former paper mill manager.

They have gathered information about Kumari, including her background as an orphan from Chennai with no family. This new information has led them to focus their investigation on Kumari, starting with the orphanage where she was raised.

The next steps for Ranjit and his team could involve interviewing staff and others associated with the orphanage to gather more information about Kumari's background, any connections she may have had, and where she could be currently located. This information could potentially lead them to John's location and shed more light on his motivations and actions.

During the interrogation, Ranjit and his team would likely ask the orphanage staff about Kumari's background, any known associates or friends, and any information they have about her connection with John. They may also ask if Kumari had shown any signs of criminal behavior while she was at the orphanage. The team would be looking for any leads that could help them track down John and Kumari and uncover their involvement in the jewelry robbery.

Ranjit and his team got a new lead about Kumari's friend named Satya Lakshmi who was believed to be involved in the robbery at the jewelry museum. When they interrogated the staff at the orphanage, they were shown an album where they saw a picture of Satya Lakshmi. However, Ranjit discovered that Satya Lakshmi was Fathima, who was believed to be the key person involved in the robbery.

Upon leaving the orphanage, Ranjit and his team went to Fathima's room to interrogate her, but she was not there. Her roommate told them that Fathima received a call in the middle of the night two days ago and left, taking her luggage with her. The roommate also mentioned that she tried to contact Fathima, but her phone was switched off. This information was important as it provided a new lead to Ranjit and his team.

Ranjit and his team quickly traced the location of Fathima's phone and found that the last known location was at a park. They went to the park to gather more information and reviewed the CCTV footage. The footage showed John and Fathima together, with John offering her some money, but Fathima was crying and refusing to take it. Later, Kumari also arrived and was comforting Fathima. After a few minutes, all three of them left the park together. From this, Ranjit was able to deduce that all three of them were involved in the robbery together. This new information helped Ranjit and his team in their investigation and they continued to pursue the case.

Ranjit was feeling the pressure of the robbery case. He was determined to solve the case and track down the suspects, John, Kumari, and Fathima. Despite putting in several days of tireless investigation and following leads, Ranjit was unable to find any trace of the suspects. This was a first for Ranjit in his long career as a police officer. He felt like he was failing, and he was consumed by thoughts of not being able to solve the case.

As he went home, he couldn't shake the feeling of disappointment and frustration. He was distant from his family and couldn't even talk to his wife, who usually offered comfort and support. He was consumed with the case and was determined to find the suspects.

The robbery case was a significant one, and the superiors were putting pressure on Ranjit to solve it as soon as possible. The suspects could be anywhere, and time was running out. Ranjit was struggling with the thought of not being able to solve the case and potentially losing his job as a result. He felt that his entire career was on the line, and he couldn't bear the thought of failing.

Ranjit had always been a dedicated police officer, and this case was no different. However, the lack of progress was affecting him deeply. He was used to solving cases and bringing justice to the victims, but this case was proving to be a challenge like no other. He couldn't shake the feeling of failure and couldn't see a way forward.

The thought of resigning from his job was weighing heavily on Ranjit's mind. He felt like he was letting everyone down and that he was no longer fit to be a police officer. However, Ranjit knew that he couldn't give up just yet. He was determined to solve the case and find the suspects, no matter what it took. He knew that it was his duty to the victims and the public to bring the suspects to justice.

Despite the obstacles, Ranjit was not ready to give up. He knew that he had to push through and continue the investigation. He was determined to find the suspects and solve the case. With this in mind, Ranjit continued to search for new leads and investigate every possibility. He was determined to bring closure to the case and bring justice to the victims.

Ranjit was facing a difficult time in his career as a police officer. Despite the pressure from superiors and the lack of progress, he was determined to solve the case and find the suspects. He was consumed with the case and couldn't shake the feeling of failure, but he knew that he couldn't give up just yet. He was dedicated to his duty as a police officer and was determined to bring justice to the victims.

Ranjit was surprised by the sudden call from his office that the criminal, John Abraham, who was involved in the robbery case he was investigating, was arrested in Tamil Nadu's Chengalpattu district. He was stunned by the news and quickly gathered himself and got dressed to start his journey to Chengalpattu. He was determined to finally solve this case and bring the criminals to justice.

As he made his way to Chengalpattu, his mind raced with thoughts of how this turn of events would impact his investigation. He was relieved that they finally had a lead, but also concerned that they might not have all the answers they needed to solve the case completely. Nevertheless, he was determined to get to the bottom of it and bring closure to the case.

When he arrived at the Chengalpattu police station, he found his team already there, eagerly waiting for him to arrive. They were all excited to finally be able to make some headway in the case and were eager to hear what the police had to say.

The police informed Ranjit and his team that John Abraham had been arrested for the brutal murder of 10 people in the Chengalpattu district. Ranjit was shocked by this news and immediately started to question the police about the details of the murder. He was determined to find out if John was connected to the robbery case in any way and if he had any information that could help solve the case.

The police provided Ranjit and his team with all the information they had gathered so far and allowed them to speak with John. Ranjit was surprised to find that John was not very forthcoming with information, but he was determined to get the answers he needed. He used his years of experience and expertise to try to get John to open up and provide some answers.

John Abraham, the main suspect in the diamond heist case, was finally caught and brought to the police station in Chengalpattu for interrogation. Ranjit, the lead investigator, was shocked but quickly composed himself and began questioning John.

John revealed a heart-wrenching story about how he became a criminal. He lost his parents to unidentified cancer and was unable to cope with their death. He turned to smoking, drinking, and gambling, which eventually led to the loss of his job. He met Kumari in a supermarket and the two became close friends and eventually started a romantic relationship. Kumari introduced him to her friend Satya Lakshmi, whom John treated as his sister.

However, fate had other plans for John as Satya was also diagnosed with same cancer that killed his parents. They took her to several hospitals, but none could cure her. They eventually found a hospital that claimed to have a cure, but it was very expensive. The hospital offered to treat Satya in exchange for the famous Empire Diamond. John, Kumari, and Satya stole the diamond and waited for the hospital to contact them.

However, the hospital never contacted them and they realized that they were being used to steal the diamond. The hospital was in financial trouble and needed the diamond to clear its debts. Satya never received proper treatment and died. Kumari was unable to bear the loss and committed suicide.

Fueled by anger and grief, John went to the hospital and demanded the return of the diamond, but he was beaten and thrown out. He then hatched a plan to get revenge on the hospital staff and brutally killed them. Afterward, he called the police and turned himself in.

John's confession gave Ranjit and his team a better understanding of the motivations behind the heist and the events that led to the murders. They still needed to verify John's story, but they were one step closer to solving the case.

Ranjit was taken aback by the sudden turn of events as John revealed his tragic story to him. He had never expected such a truth to be behind the robbery of the precious diamond. John had lost his parents to mysterious cancer and, in the process of trying to save the life of the love of his life, he found himself entangled in the dark world of crime and deceit. He had to steal the diamond to pay for the supposed cure for his beloved's cancer, only to find out too late that it was all a scam. His lover eventually died, which drove John to his breaking point, and he went on a mission of revenge, killing those who had taken advantage of him and caused him so much pain.

As John gave his final breaths, he handed Ranjit a small box, which the detective put in his pocket without even thinking. Later, after all the necessary arrangements had been made for John's funeral, Ranjit opened the box in his office. To his surprise, it was the very diamond that they had been searching for. Ranjit realized that John had wanted to return the diamond as a way of making amends for his crimes and asking for forgiveness.

Ranjit was deeply moved by John's story and the sacrifices he had made for the people he loved. He decided to return the diamond to the museum, which was met with huge applause from his department and the public. This act of bravery and honor on Ranjit's part only added to his reputation as a top-notch officer, who not only solved the case but also showed empathy and compassion towards the criminals.

With the case finally solved, Ranjit's life took a positive turn. He was able to reconnect with his family and rediscovered the happiness and joy that he had been missing for so long. He felt that only he truly understood the pain and suffering that John had gone through, and he was glad that he could bring some closure to the tragedy by returning the diamond to its rightful place.

In conclusion, Ranjit's investigation into the diamond theft was a journey of self-discovery and redemption. He learned the importance of empathy and compassion towards those who have committed crimes, as well as the power of forgiveness. Through his efforts, he was able to bring justice to the victims and peace to the souls of the perpetrators. He became a better person and a more effective detective, and his reputation as one of the finest officers in the country was solidified.

Related Books

<u>**CBI Chronicles: The Cases of Officer Ranjit**</u>
<u>**Detective Gurunadam: The Case Files (Upcoming)**</u>
Saving India from Nuclear Doom: The Sardar Story

Saving India From Nuclear Doom: The Sardar Story

Sardar, India's most skilled spy, is about to embark on his most dangerous mission yet. A terrorist group has obtained nuclear weapons and plans to launch a devastating attack on India. With time running out, Sardar is tasked with infiltrating the group and uncovering their plans before it's too late.

As he delves deeper into the terrorist organization, Sardar realizes that the stakes are higher than he ever imagined. With the fate of millions of lives in his hands, Sardar must use all of his training and skills to prevent the attack and save India from destruction.

But with his cover threatened and the clock ticking, will Sardar be able to stop the terrorists in time? Find out in this heart-pounding espionage thriller that will keep you on the edge of your seat until the very end.

Cbi Chronicles: The Cases Of Officer Ranjit

In "CBI Chronicles: The Cases of Officer Ranjit," readers are taken on a thrilling journey through the criminal underworld of India. Officer Ranjit, a seasoned investigator with the Central Bureau of Investigation (CBI), is tasked with solving some of the country's most complex and challenging crime cases.

From murders and frauds to kidnappings and political scandals, Officer Ranjit navigates through the intricate webs of crime and deceit, using his sharp wit and instincts to uncover the truth. But with powerful enemies and hidden agendas at every turn, Ranjit must stay one step ahead of the criminals and the corrupt officials to bring justice to the victims.

As the cases unfold, readers are drawn into the world of law enforcement, where the stakes are high and the dangers are real. With its fast-paced action, compelling characters, and intricate plotlines, "CBI Chronicles: The Cases of Officer Ranjit" is a gripping crime thriller that will keep you on the edge of your seat until the very last page.

Detective Gurunadam: The Case Files

In the bustling city of Nayakpur, Detective Gurunadam is a household name. Known for his keen eye for detail and his relentless pursuit of justice, Gurunadam has solved some of the city's most notorious crimes.

But when a string of seemingly unrelated murders rocks the city, even Gurunadam is stumped. With no leads and no motive, the case seems impossible to solve. But Gurunadam refuses to give up, and as he delves deeper into the investigation, he uncovers a web of lies, secrets, and deceit that threaten to tear the city apart.

As the bodies pile up and the stakes get higher, Gurunadam must use all of his skills and experience to bring the killer to justice. But as the case becomes more complex, even Gurunadam begins to question whether he can solve this mystery before it's too late.

With its gripping plot, dynamic characters, and vivid setting, this novel is a thrilling ride through the world of crime and justice. Join Detective Gurunadam as he navigates the twists and turns of this complex case, and see if he can solve the mystery before it's too late.

Printed by Libri Plureos GmbH in Hamburg, Germany